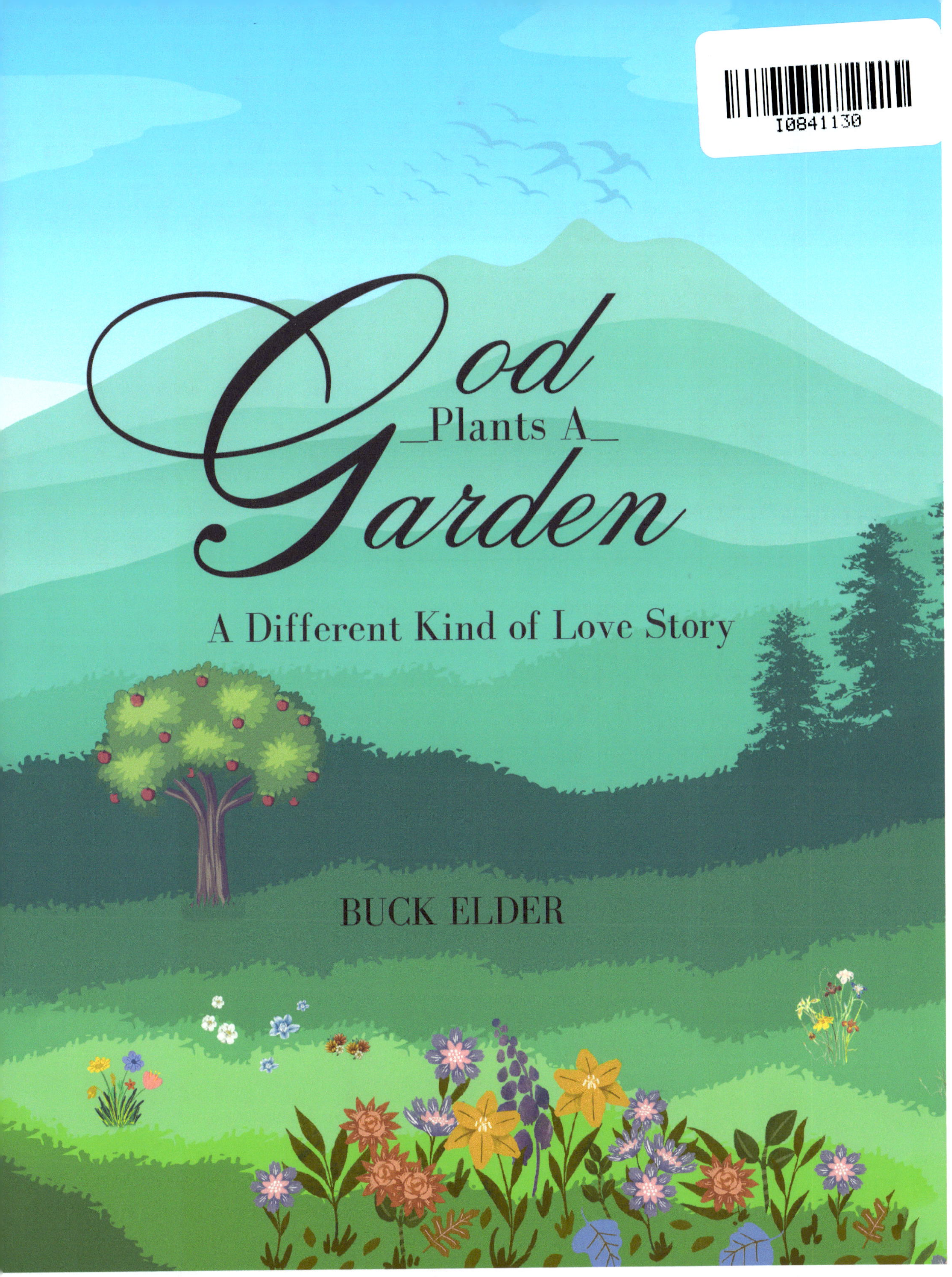
God
Plants A
Garden
A Different Kind of Love Story
BUCK ELDER

Published in the United States of America
Brilliant Books Literary
137 Forest Park Lane Thomasville
North Carolina 27360 USA

ISBN:
Paperback: 979-8-88945-265-2
Ebook: 979-8-88945-266-9
Hardback: 979-8-88945-267-6

CONTENTS

CHAPTER 1

Where Shall I Put It?

A long, long, long, long time ago, about the time that time began, God decided He wanted a garden. God enjoyed watching things grow and thought a beautiful garden would give Him a lifetime of joy and happiness, especially if He could share it with others.

Then, thought God, "What do I need to do to get started?"

"Well," God said to Himself, "first, I must have a place to put a garden."

Then God thought and thought some more. "Ah," He said, "I will create a universe. That will be a splendid place for a garden."

"But how big should the universe be? Should it be small, or medium size, or very, very large?" God pondered. "I've got it! Since I am Lord of all, the universe needs to be the largest thing that exists; large enough to hold not only My garden but everything that there is."

So God created the universe large enough to hold all that exists, and nothing would exist that was not in the universe, and only God would know where the universe started and stopped. And since the universe was so large that no one would ever be able to go from one end to the other, God decided that it was not important for anyone other than Him to know exactly how large the universe really was.

Then God looked all over His universe, first looking here then looking there, and when He found just the right spot, He said, "That's the perfect place. That's where I'll put My garden."

Thus, the beginning had begun.

CHAPTER 2

What Should It Look Like?

"Next," pondered God, "now that I have a place to put My garden, what should it look like? Should it be long and narrow, short and wide, thick or thin? Should it be shallow or deep, flat or hilly, square or round?

"Decisions, decisions, decisions, so many decisions to make. One would think planning a garden would not involve so many decisions. Well, let's see, at the spot I have picked out I believe I will start with a barren, lifeless, shapeless form covered in large part with water and sitting in the dark. I think it will be just right."

But God did not want this to be just any ordinary garden. It was going to be God's garden, a very special garden like no other place in the universe. So to let it be known how special this garden was to be, God let His spirit move across the waters to bless His creation and proclaim His dominion over all that existed.

Then God thought, "I have just got to get around to deciding about a shape. Ah, that's it." God said, "I will make My garden round, like a ball. That would be the very best shape so that the garden can have the most surface area."

"But what do I need to do to this ball so that it will be a good garden for growing things?" thought God. "Should it have a soft center and hard surface, or should the middle be hard and the surface soft? Does it need to be wet or dry? Does the outside need to be smooth or bumpy? Does the surface need to be the same all over, or should some of it be one way and other parts another way? Should it be hot or cold or just warm? What would be the best to grow things in?"

Just like us, God also had some challenging decisions to make. But God always knows best, and He reasoned that soft dirt would be needed on top in which to grow things, but a strong, hard core, like rock, under the dirt would be needed so that the ball would keep its shape. God also figured that the hard rock underneath would help keep things in place on the top, because if the whole ball was soft, everything on the surface of the garden might fall or sink into the center. Wasn't God clever!

So God took the rock, clay, and dirt that existed within the shapeless form at the spot He had selected for his garden, and with His mighty hands, He formed a ball. Then God thought, "What should I call this kind of ball-shaped garden that is sitting out in the middle of all this space that I have created? Let's see, if this is going to be a good garden, I will eventually have to plant things in it, and when I am finished, everything that will be planted will have been planted by Me."

"That's it!" God said to Himself. "I will call my ball-shaped garden a *planet* since I will be the one to plant it."

CHAPTER 3

I Need Some Light Down Here

Now that God had made a place to put His garden and shaped His garden into a ball, He realized that the garden could not be seen very well because it was still dark all around.

"What can I do," God pondered, "so My garden can be better seen?"

"Ah," thought God, "light would be good. What a bright idea!"

So God decided to create light, and He said, "Let there be light." And light came forth just as God commanded it to. However, it was not light from any far-off place, but rather, it was light created by God simply by Him ordering light to appear; a more permanent light source was to come later. God saw that the light was good and that it was good for the garden.

Then God realized that He had both light and darkness, and although both were good, the garden would grow better if He kept the darkness away from the light and the light away from the darkness.

Thus, God decided to separate the darkness from the light so that wherever there was darkness, there would be no light, and where there was light, there would be no darkness. Just think about what God did. He fixed it so that light and total darkness could never be in the same place at the same time. God made it that way from the beginning, and it's been the same ever since.

CHAPTER 4

Good Morning and Good Night

"I'm still working on the first day and there are still more decisions to be made, including what to call the light and the dark" thought God to Himself. That's it! A great name for the light would be *day*. But what should I call the dark?" "Let's see," as God continued to consider the matter, "dark is the same as *no light*. How about combining the words *no* and *light*? That's it! I will combine *no* and *light* and call the darkness *night*."

And then God's garden had both day and night.

"So," God pondered, "now that I have light and dark, what should I call the time when the light is just about to go away and darkness is just about to take over, that time when the amount of light is about even with the amount of darkness? Let Me see, since the light and darkness will be almost even, I'll call this time *evening*."

"But," thought God, "I also need a name for the time when light takes over again and darkness goes away. I know! Because when the light starts to shine and take over, the light will be *more in* the garden than the darkness, I will call this time *morning*."

Then God put His hands on His hips and looked around. "Not a bad job for the first day's work. Everything looks pretty good so far."

So God finished the first day of work on His garden, and He saw that what He had done was good.

CHAPTER 5

Give Me Some Air

"Well," thought God as He began working in His garden the second day, "a good garden will need lots of air. Now let's see, there is so much water in My garden spot, how am I going to get air to it, and where should I put the air?"

After pondering the situation for a moment, God decided to create a giant superdome over the garden. God then thought, "What name should I give to this dome?" "I know," God concluded, "because the top of the dome is going to be so high, I will take the words *so* and *high*, blend them together, and call this dome the *sky*."

Then, as though parting a great sea, God made some of the water rise up into the sky like a giant cloud, covering the entire garden. The rest of the water God left below on the garden.

"Now," said God, "I can put the air under the dome so that it will separate the water, which is on my garden down below, from the water that I have placed up in the sky, and I will save all the water I have stored in the sky above in case I need it for a rainy day."

Day 2 had now drawn to a close, and God liked what He had done so far, and saw that it was good.

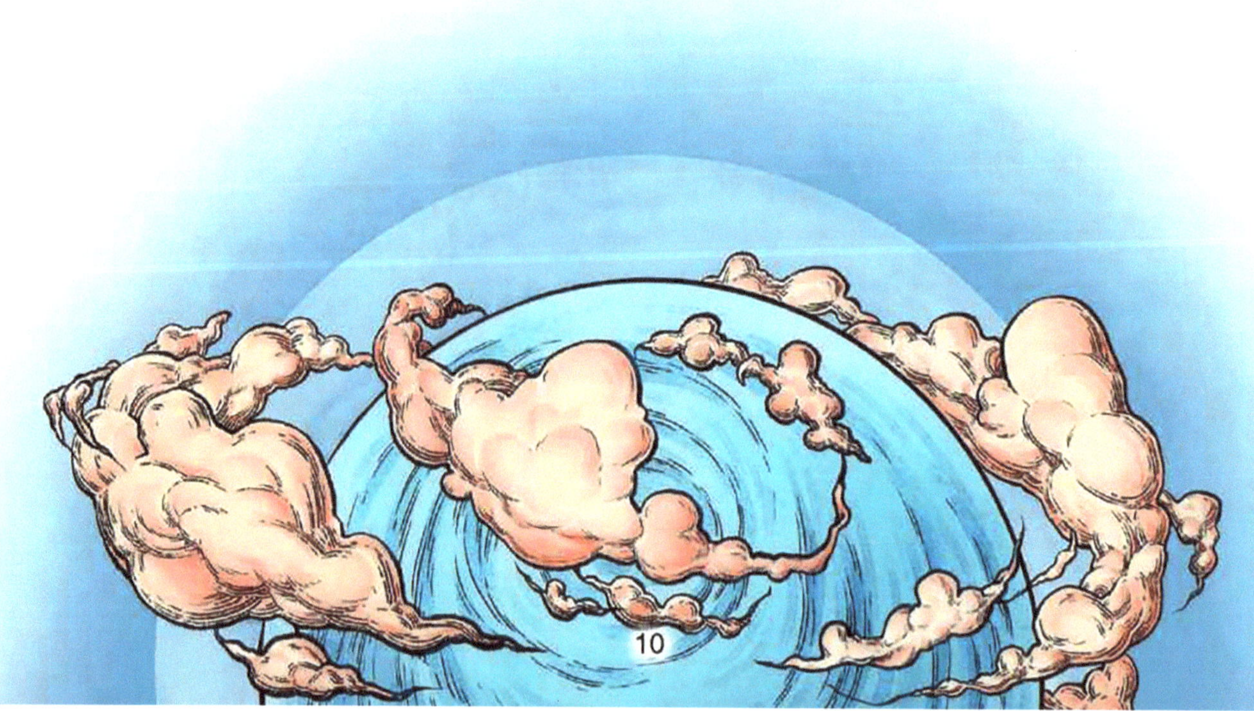

CHAPTER 6

So Where Would Be the Best Place to Watch My Garden Grow?

"Now that I have selected a shape for My garden and the materials needed to make it and have given it some air, where would be the best place for Me to be so I can watch My garden grow?" God asked Himself.

"I could find a good spot in the garden and just always sit there," God thought. "But if I sit in just one place, I would not be able to see the entire garden all the time," God reasoned. "What I really need," God thought, "is a place where I can be close, but not so far away that I would not be able to reach down to the garden to take care of it and all the things living and growing there."

"Aha!" God exclaimed. "Up above the sky would be ideal! This would be a good place where I can watch over the whole garden all at once and see everything that happens in it, and that would also be a good place for Me to call home."

And in this place God selected to make His home would be *He, even* while He was also watching over His garden. So God decided to blend the words *he* and *even* together and name His home *heaven*.

But then God reasoned that sitting up in heaven would still not be the same as actually being in the garden. Then it came to God. "I am God and I can always be everywhere, so not only could I be in a place up high where I can always see My garden, but because I am God, I can also be ever-present in My garden to take care of the things in it whenever they need Me."

So God decided that to best take care of His creation, He would always be both in heaven and down in His garden, and that way He could both enjoy His garden and care for the living things in it all at the same time.

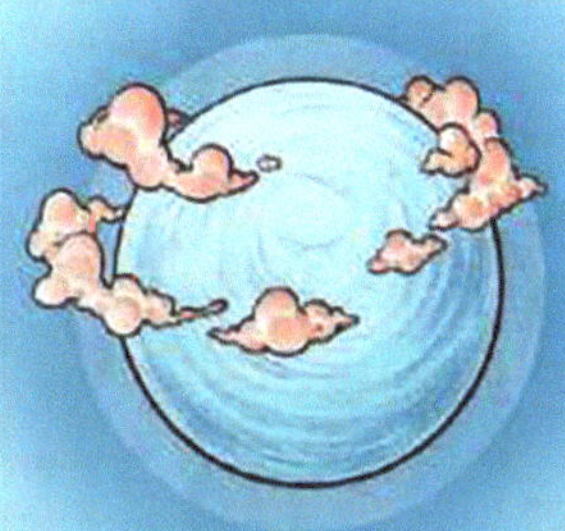

CHAPTER 7

Water, Water Everywhere

"Well," thought God, "what should I do next? Let's see. I've got a place for My garden, I have shaped it like a ball, and I have already watered it well. In fact, I've got water everywhere. But I know I still need some dry dirt on the surface in which things can grow."

So God decided to separate the water from the dirt and to reshape the surface of the big ball garden He had created. He first scooped out some large, deep holes and caused most of the water to roll off the dirt into those large holes, and God called some of those large holes oceans and others He called seas. God also decided to make some smaller holes and ditches of various sizes to hold the water that wouldn't fit into the oceans and seas. He called these smaller holes lakes and ponds. The large ditches God called rivers, the medium-size ditches He called streams, and the smaller ditches He called creeks; and God used the rivers, streams, and creeks to take the water off the dirt to both the large and small holes He had dug.

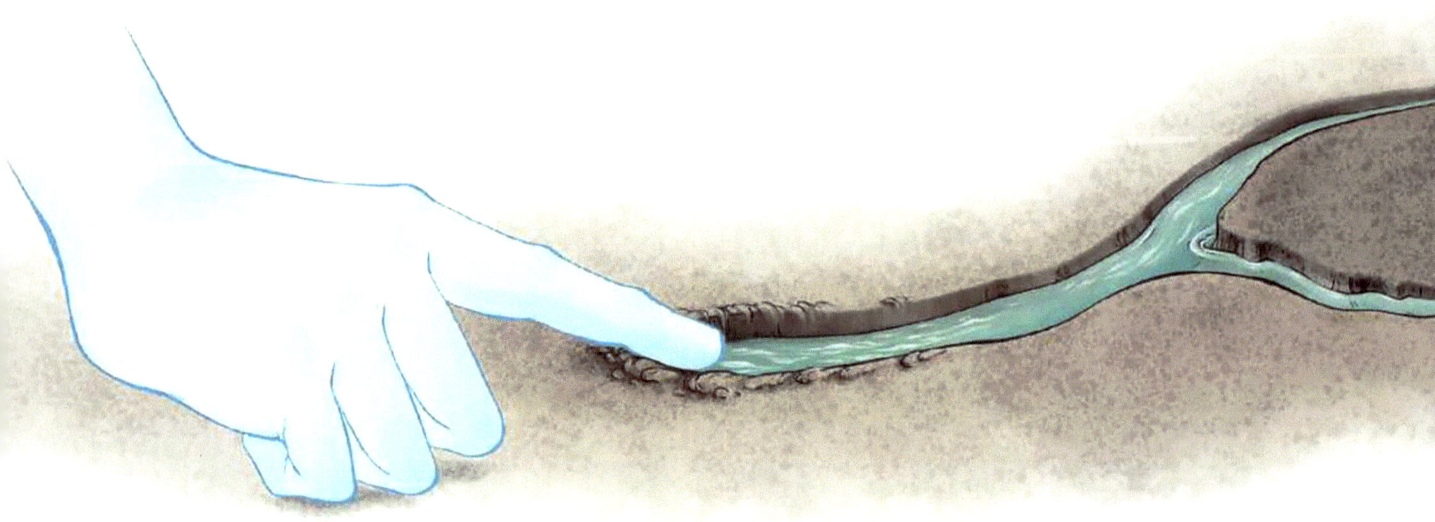

God then looked around at the dirt that He had dug from the holes and began to scratch His head trying to determine what He should do with it. "I've got it," He thought. "I'll pile the dirt around on the dry parts of the garden at different locations to make hills, then I will put most of the sand in places that I'll call deserts, and I will also spread some of the sand along the edges of the oceans and seas to use for places I will call beaches. To provide even more variety, I will cause some rock to rise up from the center of the big ball in various places to make mountains of all shapes and sizes. And I shall call the dry parts of my garden *land* because it has been made with the *Lord's hand.* And the dry dirt I have made to plant things in, I shall call *earth.*"

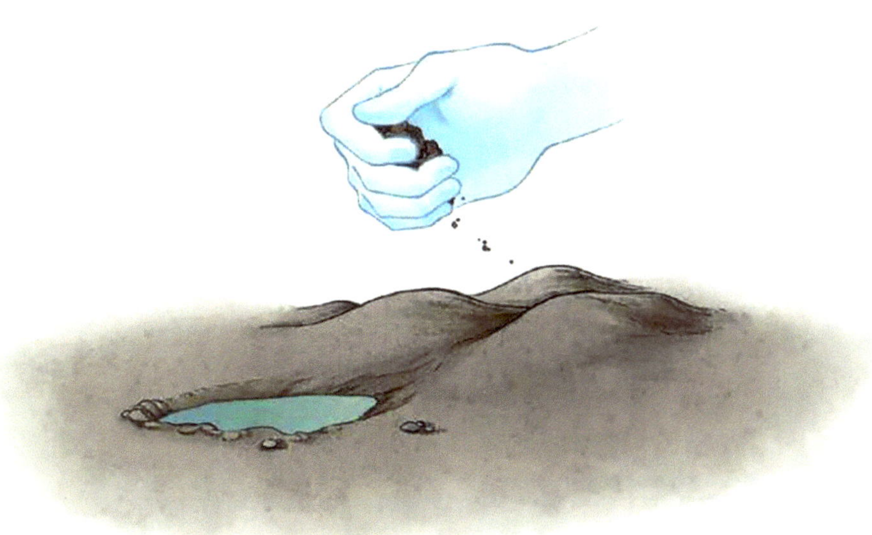

And God was very pleased with what He had done.

But then God said to Himself, "I think My garden would be much more interesting if the dry land is laid out in different shapes and sizes."

So God proceeded to spread out the land and shape it into all sorts of pieces, some large, some small, some medium in size. Some pieces He made into islands of all designs and sizes, while other pieces He made into giant continents. And no two pieces of land were the same size or exactly alike.

And God looked around and said, "I like this. My garden is really starting to take shape."

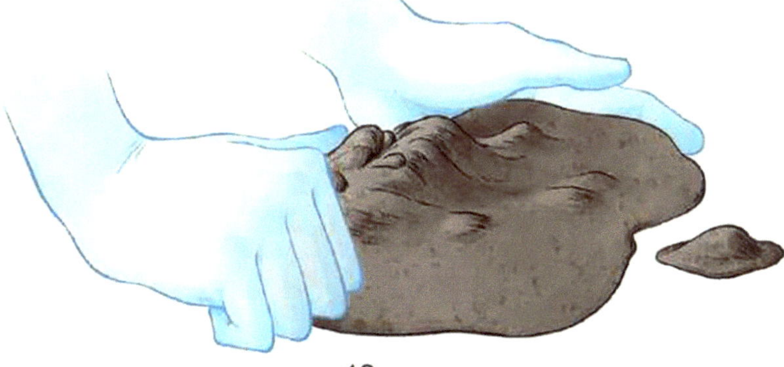

CHAPTER 8

Who Wants Some Veggies?

"Okay, I've now gotten my garden spot ready, but what do I put in it first?" God asked Himself. "Well," He thought, "how about some vegetation? That will look nice. But I don't want all of it to be the same size or color or just alike."

"I think what I'll do is plant all sorts of living vegetation, some big and tall, some small and spread out, some thick and others thin, some hard and some soft, and a lot in between. I'll let some vegetation have just seeds while others will have fruit with seeds inside, and the vegetation can use the seed to reproduce and grow more of its own kind and also provide food for other living things I may put in my garden later." So God planted the vegetation and seed He had made. Then God said, "Because I have planted these living things Myself, I will call them *plants*."

So God watched the vegetation he had planted grow from the earth, and He saw it make seed and fruit with seeds inside, and God was very pleased because all this was good.

Then God looked about His garden and thought, "I should also make plants with lots of pretty colors to brighten the garden and to bring smiles and happiness to the other things I will put there. Some of these pretty colors I shall call flowers. And the flowers shall also bear seeds that can be spread by the wind and other things I shall put on the land."

Before He knew it, God had finished the third day working on His garden, and He said to Himself, "This is good so far, but I am only halfway through. It looks like I still have about three more days of work left to do."

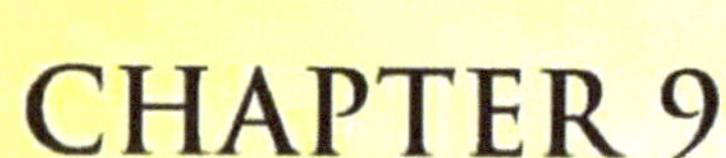

CHAPTER 9

Great Ball of Fire

"You know," God said, talking out loud to Himself the next morning, "the idea of light is good, but I think I need to replace the first light I made the other day with a permanent light source that will keep burning all the time and that will help warm the land and help the things in My garden grow."

"But what can I use to provide all the light that will be needed for My garden not only for now but forever?" thought God.

"I know!" God shouted to Himself. "I will make a great ball of fire and let it shine down on My garden, but only for part of the time. It will be difficult for the things in My garden to rest if the light shines all the time."

"Oh yeah!" God again exclaimed to Himself. "Since that ball of fire will have to be very, very big and very, very hot, I better put it far enough away from My garden so it won't make the garden too hot and burn it up, but at the same time, that light also needs to be close enough to the garden to keep the things in it from getting too cold."

So God figured out exactly how far away to put the great ball of fire so it would be just the right distance from the garden to make it warm enough for things to live in it but not so hot to burn them up.

Wow, it must have taken a lot of know-how to figure exactly how to make a ball of fire big enough to do all that and where to put it and how to keep it burning all by itself forever without burning out. God really must be some kind of genius!

"Now," thought God, "since I've created this great ball of fire, I need to come up with a name for it."

"I have it!" God said. "Since My son is the brightest thing in My life, and since this ball of fire will be the brightest thing in the life of My garden, I will call this ball of fire the *sun*."

CHAPTER 10

Night-Lights

"But this still does not solve all My problems," God thought to Himself. "Even though My garden may need some rest from the sunlight during the nighttime, I still want to be able to see My garden at night and let the things in My garden know that I am still watching over them even when it is dark. So what do I need?"

"Aha! A big night-light with some smaller night-lights scattered about would be just the thing! These night-lights shouldn't be too bright, but they should give off just enough light in My garden so there will not be total darkness."

"Now, where should I put these night-lights? Let Me see, I think I will put the big night-light closer to My garden than the sun, but instead of making another ball of fire like the sun, I will just let the sun bounce its light off a large round rock. By doing this, My big night-light will only provide a soft, glowing light for the garden during the darkness but will not make any heat like the sun."

"And what should I call the large light at night? Let's see," pondered God. "When the sun is at its highest point in the sky, it is noon, and the opposite of noon is the middle of the night, which I shall call midnight. So if I let My largest night-light shine its brightest and be close to its highest point at midnight, it would be like a *midnight noon*. Thus, I think I will take the first letter from *midnight* and combine it with the last three letters of *noon* and call this large night-light the *moon*."

"And what about the smaller night-lights? Where should I put them, and what should I call them?" God again pondered as He looked around His garden. "Let Me see. I think I will make these small lights so they will be like scattered twinklers and radiating sparklers—but that's too big a name for small lights. I think I will shorten the name by just using the first letter from each word, S-T-A-R-S, and I will call these smaller lights *stars*.

"But unlike the moon, which will be close to the garden, I will let the stars be brighter but much farther away. In fact, I will put them so far away that they will not appear to move in the night sky. By doing this, the stars will give My garden and the things in it a sense of security at night. I will let the stars seem to remain almost stationary, and perhaps they can be used to help determine where things are located in My garden or used to serve as points of reference. I may even arrange some of the stars to look like pictures in the night sky and even come up with some other uses for them, but only I will know what is written in the stars."